ANIMAL
CRACKERS

★ TINY TIM ★

ROSE IMPEY ★ SHOO RAYNER

ORCHARD BOOKS
338 Euston Road, London NW1 3BH
Orchard Books Australia
Hachette Children's Books
Level 17/207 Kent Street, Sydney NSW 2000

First published by Orchard Books in 1993
This edition published in 2009

Text © Rose Impey 1993
Illustrations © Shoo Rayner 2002

The rights of Rose Impey to be identified as the author and
Shoo Rayner to be identified as the illustrator of this Work
have been asserted by them in accordance with the
Copyright, Designs and Patents Act, 1988.

A CIP catalogue record for this book is available from the British Library.

ISBN 978 1 40830 508 9

1 3 5 7 9 10 8 6 4 2
Printed in China

Orchard Books is a division of Hachette Children's Books,
an Hachette UK company.
www.hachette.co.uk

Tiny Tim

Frogs can jump.
Everybody knows that.
But how far, that's the question?

It was the middle of May.
The whole town was getting ready
for the Jumping Jubilee.
Everywhere frogs were training
for the big jump.

There were frogs leaping over lakes,

hurtling over houses,

shooting out of shops

and catapulting over car parks.

Everywhere you looked
frogs were flying through the air.

"There's going to be an accident,"
said the chief of police.
But no one listened.
Even the mayor was too busy
jumping over a traffic jam.

The champion jumper
was Rosie the Ribeter.
She had won the Jumping Jubilee
five times.

She could jump six and a half metres.
It was a record.

Even Fanny, the Flying Phenomenon,
couldn't beat Rosie.

Rosie was big, for a frog.
She was from a big family.
She had three big brothers
and a big sister.
And a big mum and dad.
They all helped to run
the Jumping Jubilee.

Her big brother Robbie
took the money.

Her big brother Ricky
announced the jumps.

Her big brother Raymond measured the jumps.

And her big sister Roseanne made the tea.

Rosie's mum and dad just watched.
Mostly, they liked to watch
Rosie win.
No matter how hard
the other frogs tried
Rosie *always* won.
She was the best –
up to now.

But there was one frog
who thought he could beat her.
His name was Tiny Tim.
He was really tiny.
But you should have seen him jump!

Tiny Tim had been jumping
since he was born.
As soon as he was out of his cot,
he jumped over it.

He jumped over his desk at school.
He nearly jumped over the school.

And he didn't only do high jumps.
He could do long jumps too.

Tiny Tim had set his heart
on winning the Jumping Jubilee.

But each time he tried
they wouldn't let him in.
"How old are you?" said Robbie.
"Five," said Tiny Tim.
"Five! Is that all?" said Robbie.
"You have to be six to jump.
That is the rule.

And rules are rules.
Now, hop it, baby face."

Robbie was a *big* frog
so Tiny Tim hopped it.

The next year Tiny Tim tried again.
"I'm six now," he said,
"and I want to jump."
"No chance," said Robbie.

"No spotty frogs allowed.
That is the rule.
And rules are rules.
Clear off, spotty."

Robbie was a *big* frog
so Tiny Tim cleared off.

Next year Tiny Tim tried again.
This time he was striped –
red and green.
"Haven't I seen you before?"
said Robbie.
"I'm seven and I'm striped,"
said Tiny Tim, "and I want to jump."
"You're a boy," said Robbie.

"No boys allowed.
That is the rule.
And rules are rules.
Now, get lost, laddie."

Robbie was a *big* frog
so Tiny Tim got lost.

The next time Tiny Tim tried,
all his family came with him –
and all his friends.
"My name is Tammy," he lied.
"I'm eight years old,
I'm a striped frog
and I want to jump. Now!"

"That's right," said all his family
and all his friends.
"Tammy wants to jump!"

NOW!

"OK! OK!" said Robbie.
"No problem. Come right in.
Everybody welcome."
Robbie was a big frog
but he wasn't *that* big.

At last, Ricky announced
the main jump.

Take your place
for the Triple Jump Final.

Tiny Tim took his place.

"First long jumper –
Rosie the Ribeter," said Ricky.
"On your marks. Get set. Go!"

"Ribet. Ribet. Ribet," said Rosie.
Rosie jumped one – two – three.

She jumped six metres fifty-five!
It was a good jump.
It was a new record.
The crowd cheered.

Next came Fanny, the Flying
Phenomenon.

Well done!

She jumped one – two – three.
She jumped six metres exactly.
It was a good jump,
but not good enough.
The crowd cheered,
but not as loud.

Good try!

Then Tiny Tim jumped.
The crowd couldn't believe their eyes.
He almost flew through the air.
He jumped one – two – three.

Raymond measured it.
Tiny Tim jumped ten metres three!

Raymond measured it again,
and again. But he couldn't
make it shorter. Tiny Tim had won.
The crowd cheered and stamped
their feet.

Rosie didn't cheer.
Nor did Rosie's family.
"You can't win," said Rosie.
"Why not?" said Tiny Tim.
"You're too small."

"*Too small?*" said Tiny Tim.
"How tall are you?" said Rosie.
"Seven and a half centimetres,"
said Tiny Tim.
"All jumping frogs must be
ten centimetres tall," said Rosie.
"That is the rule," said Robbie.
"And rules are rules."

Robbie and Ricky and Raymond
and Roseanne and their
mum and dad cheered.
"Rosie's the winner,"
Ricky announced.

"That's not fair," said Tiny Tim.
"That's the rule," said Ricky.
"Hop it, shorty."
Ricky was a *very big* frog.
He was the biggest in the family.

But now Tiny Tim was mad.
He was so mad he started to puff up.
He puffed up his chest.

He puffed up his stomach.

He puffed up his cheeks.

He stood on his tiptoes.

Tiny Tim grew and grew and grew.
He looked as if he might burst.
"Now…measure me," he said.
"Go on, measure him," said all his
family and all his friends.
Raymond measured him.

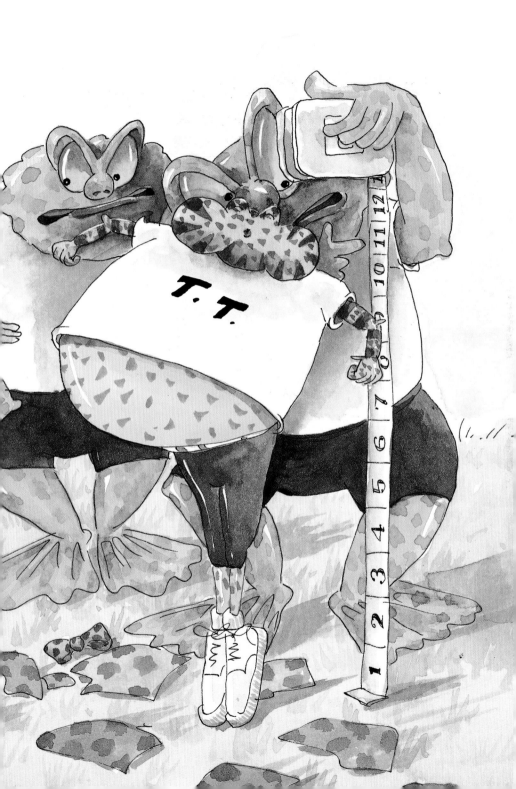

"Ten centimetres – and a half,"
said Raymond.

"All right, you win," said Rosie.
"I know when I'm beaten."

Tiny Tim stopped growing.
"Tiny Tim is the winner," said Ricky.
"He is the champion."
The crowd cheered and stamped
their feet.

Hooray!

"Next year," said Tiny Tim,
"because I am the champion
I will make the rules.
And the only rule will be
'*no more rules*'!"

Crack-A-Joke

What goes *dot-dot-dot, croak?*
A morse toad!

What do frogs like to eat?
Lolly hops!

What's brown on the outside, green on the inside, and hops?
A frog sandwich!

What do frogs like to drink?
Croak-a-Cola!

TOAD-IN-THE-HOLE

Where does a frog hang up his hat and coat?

In the croakroom.

ANIMAL
CRACKERS

COLLECT ALL THE
ANIMAL CRACKERS BOOKS!

A Birthday for Bluebell	978 1 40830 293 4	£4.99
Too Many Babies	978 1 40830 294 1	£4.99
Hot Dog Harris	978 1 40830 295 8	£4.99
Sleepy Sammy	978 1 40830 296 5	£4.99
Precious Potter	978 1 40830 297 2	£4.99
Phew Sidney	978 1 40830 298 9	£4.99
Open Wide Wilbur	978 1 40830 299 6	£4.99
We Want William	978 1 40830 300 9	£4.99
Welcome Home, Barney!	978 1 40830 513 3	£4.99
A Medal For Poppy	978 1 40830 510 2	£4.99
A Fortune For Yo-Yo	978 1 40830 509 6	£4.99
Long Live Roberto	978 1 40830 512 6	£4.99
Rhode Island Roy	978 1 40830 514 0	£4.99
Tiny Tim	978 1 40830 508 9	£4.99
Pipe Down, Prudle!	978 1 40830 511 9	£4.99
Stella's Staying Put	978 1 40830 515 7	£4.99

All priced at £4.99

Orchard Colour Crunchies are available from all good bookshops, or can be
ordered direct from the publisher:
Orchard Books, PO BOX 29, Douglas IM99 1BQ
Credit card orders please telephone 01624 836000
or fax 01624 837033 or visit our internet site: www.orchardbooks.co.uk
or e-mail: bookshop@enterprise.net for details.
To order please quote title, author and ISBN
and your full name and address.
Cheques and postal orders should be made payable to 'Bookpost plc.'
Postage and packing is FREE within the UK
(overseas customers should add £2.00 per book).
Prices and availability are subject to change.